Bonesy and Isabel

Michael J. Rosen

Illustrated by
James Ransome

Harcourt Brace & Company

San Diego   New York   London

Requests for permission to make copies of any part of the work should
be mailed to: Permissions Department, Harcourt Brace & Company,
6277 Sea Harbor Drive, Orlando, Florida 32887-6777.

Library of Congress Cataloging-in-Publication Data
Rosen, Michael J., 1954–
Bonesy and Isabel/by Michael J. Rosen; illustrated by James
Ransome. — 1st ed.
p.   cm.
Summary: Isabel, an adopted Salvadoran girl, adjusts to her new life in
America by befriending the old dog Bonesy, but then she must deal with
her grief when he dies.
ISBN 0–15–209813–5
[1. Salvadoran Americans — Fiction. 2. Adoption — Fiction. 3. Dogs —
Fiction. 4. Death — Fiction.]   I. Ransome, James, ill.
II. Title.
PZ7.R71868Bo   1995
[E] — dc20   93-7892

Printed in Singapore

First edition

A B C D E

The illustrations in this book were done in oil paint
on Arches watercolor paper.
The display type was set in Barcelona by Thompson Type,
San Diego, California.
The text type was set in Stempel Garamond by Thompson Type,
San Diego, California.
Color separations by Bright Arts, Ltd., Singapore
Printed and bound by Tien Wah Press, Singapore
This book was printed with soya-based inks on Leykam recycled paper,
which contains more than 20 percent postconsumer waste and has a total
recycled content of at least 50 percent.
Production supervision by Warren Wallerstein and David Hough
Designed by Lydia D'moch

For Steven Fischer and his original Bonesy
                              —M. J. R.

To Jaime—
Thank God for you, and the angels for
your beautiful smile and those eyes
                              —J. R.

Before Isabel came to the house on Sunbury Road, thirty-five other creatures were living there. At least thirty-five — and that's not counting all the creatures that couldn't be counted. Three horses grazed the grassy fields. Eleven ducks paddled a pond that had been dug and filled only a few years earlier. Eight or nine cats prowled the place — some inside and some outside. And nine dogs called that house their home: all outside dogs that used to be strays (mixed-up breeds and many sizes), except for one inside dog, a twelve-year-old Labrador retriever named Bonesy.

And then there were two people who cared for all these countable creatures. They were the ones who had brought Isabel from El Salvador.

The main house on Sunbury Road had once been a cabin, but over the years, the many owners had made one addition after another. Now there are fifteen rooms, as well as a pair of barns, gardens in all the sunny and partly sunny spots, a tool shed, an empty corncrib, timber and picket fences, part of a pine forest, a deck, and a pasture, too. The whole place rambles like a long story. And each creature who lives in or around or above the house on Sunbury Road knows a different part of that story.

The barn swallows and nighthawks could tell you about the chimney smoke and the antenna's perches, where the roof slates have cracked and the gutters have clogged with leaves.

The horses know the barnyard's circles, the mole and rabbit holes in the fields, the scrambling gravel along the roads, and how far it is from here to most anywhere.

The cats spy on everyone, nosing into nooks and niches where crickets *chirr* and mice skedattle. Still, whatever stories the cats discover they don't tell a living soul.

But the nine dogs in Isabel's new house share a single story. It's the story of the people who took them from the dangerous roads where each had been abandoned. Of course, they all know the faint wind's gossip of scents and the story of the fences where they bark to passersby: *Don't bother our house*. Yet the real story they like to tell is about the people of the house who speak to them in a strange language — words that, most of the time, just mean, *We care for you*.

When Isabel came to the house, she knew only a few words of that strange language, English — about as much as the dogs knew, which was a lot more than the horses would ever know, and a little more than the cats admitted knowing. As for the uncountable birds, Isabel quickly learned the nighthawks' *peent*, *peent*, and the swallows' rapid *tat-tat-tat-tat*.

And so Isabel spent her summer listening to the animals who showed her all they knew about the place. Though she didn't understand their busy language, it sounded good to her. The animals of Sunbury Road spoke like the wandering mules and chickens and goats from the roads of El Salvador Isabel remembered.

Isabel called the people who lived in the house "Vera" and "Ivan." They were the ones who groomed the horses, flea-dipped the cats, untangled burrs from the dogs' coats, and stuffed the bird feeders with suet. They were the ones who had brought Isabel from a country farther away than any of the resident birds could report from their high-up views.

People were always visiting Isabel's new house — especially at dinnertime when there would be clinking glasses and clouds of laughter. Although Isabel couldn't often understand what was funny, she at least understood that Vera and Ivan and their friends were happy. Laughing in English sounded just like laughing in Spanish.

It was Bonesy, the one inside dog, who became Isabel's closest companion. Isabel even recognized the word "companion" the first time Vera pronounced it slowly; it sounded so much like *compañero*. Bonesy was allowed inside because he was old. And because he had lost most of his teeth, he was allowed to eat table scraps. And because he had arthritis, Bonesy was even allowed to stay under the dining room table, where scraps could be slipped to him under the tablecloth. He never begged. He just waited — or slept. While Vera and Ivan and their guests would laugh, Isabel would feed Bonesy the soft leftovers from her plate. She would slip off her shoes and stroke Bonesy's coat with her bare toes.

And so it was the always-awaiting Bonesy who helped Isabel study English. A little of it, anyway. Under the dining room table with the sleepy dog, Isabel would sound out the English words in her new books. Though Bonesy didn't know if it was right when Isabel said *hor-SES* or when she said *HOR-ses*, he rewarded her with licks just for practicing beside him. The warm breeze from Bonesy's nose would riffle the pages of her book. And whenever Isabel said *Bonesy* or *Good dog!* or *¡Perro bueno!*, the old retriever would thump his tail against the rug. Whatever language Isabel spoke, Bonesy seemed to know she was saying what his other humans often said: *I care for you*.

One evening, Vera and Ivan invited another family of three to dinner. Isabel helped set the table with freshly ironed linens, with plates that someone in a nearby town had made from clay, and with flowers she had helped Ivan gather from the horses' field. Earlier in the day she had picked peaches from their own trees and rolled out a pie crust with Vera. She learned a word or two with each of these little jobs.

The guests, Mr. and Mrs. Jeffrey and their daughter Emmie, sat directly across the table from Ivan and Vera and Isabel. Of course, Bonesy, to whom everyone was introduced, slept among the six pairs of feet.

Dinner began with Vera's minty soup and lots of words that Isabel hadn't studied. She slipped off her shoes and began to stroke Bonesy with her toes. Emmie passed Isabel the basket of chewy bread that her family had brought, and Isabel nudged Bonesy with her foot to offer him a piece from which she had torn the crust. Once the dinner plates arrived, Isabel peeked under the table and saw the bread still lying beside her shoe. Then someone pronounced the words for her old country, *El Salvador*, and this made her smile. Emmie repeated the words and smiled back at Isabel, and then, because Emmie didn't know any other Spanish, she turned back to her plate and began to arrange her green beans into rows.

Throughout dinner, Bonesy ignored Isabel's offer of a green bean, a chunk of potato, and even a piece of chicken skin. Isabel wiggled her toes on Bonesy's back, nudged him, lifted his sleepy tail from the floor with her foot. While everyone at the table continued to laugh and tell stories, Isabel slid slowly off her chair and ducked beneath the tablecloth.

On her hands and knees — on all fours like Bonesy — Isabel whispered the dog's name and then said, "*¡Despiètate!* — Wake up!" But Bonesy didn't rouse, didn't lick Isabel's face, didn't wag his tail, didn't smell the chicken on her fingertips. She held her hand in front of his nose but couldn't feel the little drafts of warm air.

Isabel reached over to the dress covering Vera's knees and tugged its hem until Vera poked her head beneath the table and whispered, "What's wrong?" When Isabel pointed to Bonesy, Vera slid under the tablecloth, crawled over to the dog on her hands and knees, on all fours, and placed her hands softly on Bonesy's chest. After a quiet moment, Isabel could see Vera's eyes brimming, too, as if their tears were words that Isabel and Vera shared. Vera put one arm around Isabel and her other arm around the retriever.

Before Vera could say a word, Ivan peered under the table and saw his wife and Isabel hugging old Bonesy. He said "Excuse me" to the Jeffreys and slid under the tablecloth, creeping on all fours to join the family circle. He looked at his dog of twelve years, his wife of twenty-two years, and this beautiful girl — his new daughter — who had been living with them these last three weeks. Isabel waited for him to say something, but Ivan just shook his head as if to show her that this sadness had no translation other than their tears.

At the table, the Jeffreys looked at one another and picked at the cold remains of their dinners. Finally, Mr. Jeffrey lifted the edge of the tablecloth and peered beneath. "Can we join the fun?" he asked.

Isabel and Vera and Ivan turned to look at Mr. Jeffrey's sideways face; his smile quickly vanished.

"I'm afraid we've had a death in the family," Vera said.

Isabel could now hear gentler words outside the tablecloth and then the sound of three chairs scooting away from the table. She smelled the peach pie in the kitchen and heard the jingling of one of the outside dogs' collar tags. Isabel knew there must be English words for what she felt, but the two new people on either side of her were just as quiet as she was, as if they, too, had just arrived without English in this suddenly sad place from a faraway country.

Then the front door closed, and Isabel heard the gravel skitter along the road. But under the tablecloth, where the four of them huddled together, it was as silent as when Bonesy slept there all by himself.

A little later, the world outside the tablecloth would begin again — all the words for "clearing the table" or "feeding the animals" or "washing the dishes" — but that hadn't begun just yet. For now, three people shared a story about a house on Sunbury Road where a retriever named Bonesy had lived. It was a story that didn't need words — a long story and a happy story and a story with a quiet ending.

And then "a little later" arrived. It was, of course, waiting for them right there in the dining room. It was as shy and unexpected as another stray dog, and it needed them — as Bonesy had. It needed Vera and Ivan and Isabel. And so Isabel helped to welcome this next part of the story into her family's house.

Later still, in the light of the summer stars, Isabel helped Vera and Ivan bury Bonesy beside a tree near the old barn. And in the days that followed, Isabel shared the story of Bonesy's death with each of the animals who lived on Sunbury Road. She told her story to the outside dogs, to the in- and outside cats, to the horses, and even to the swallows and nighthawks who didn't sit still and listen. In their different languages, each of the animals understood this new friend Isabel, and they helped her practice the strange language that mostly means, *We care for you*.

M-52658

E
ROS

Rosen, Michael J.

Bonesy and Isabel

$15.00

M-52658

E
ROS

Rosen, Michael
J.

Bonesy and
Isabel

$15.00

DATE	BORROWER'S NAME	
	Relly Burnap	
NO 25 '96	IR Kristen	

BAKER & TAYLOR